FANGS OF FURY:

The Fallen Light

To my little monster Carma who can rip up a chew toy in less than an hour.

THE CLIFFS

SKY-ALPHA

BEAR-BETA

<u>**WOLVES**</u>

FOOT

GRAVEL

ICE

SORREL

RAIN

MAPLE

OWL

STORM

<u>**PHIS**</u>

DAWN

PSI

FLORAL

THORN

PUPS

LAKE

RUBBLE

PINE

FEATHER

GAMMAS

BLAZE

BLOSSOM

OAT

Prologue

Freezing air breezed on mountain tops. Snow covered the ground as thunder pounded the sky. Suddenly, a flash of fire blazed the ground.

"Stop this nonsense at once!" barked the wolf in the distance. Its glowing white fur lit up the sky. Two more wolves appeared behind her. The first wolf was unusually blue with white eyes. The second wolf was orange with solid green eyes and flame like ears.

"Why so upset?" the dark wolf taunted. Her fur was not glowing like the others. It was pitch black and she had purple eyes filled with no emotion. "Sun, sisters, I'm just doing what's best for the Valley."

"What you're doing is breaking the balance," Sun growled. Her claws sinking into the undergrowth.

"We need four comets in the sky!" Barked the blue wolf. Her voice silent. She followed Sun to face her sister.

"River is right, Moon," barked the orange wolf. "We need to work together to protect the wolves of

The Valley." She stepped up next to Sun, just like River.

"Why are you making this so hard Flame? All you have to do is let me take your element and I'll leave you alone," Moon explained. "for now." Moon suddenly disappeared into darkness and reappeared behind Sun. She clawed at her white scruff. River's eyes filled with rage as she dragged Moon off Sun.

"We don't want to fight you," River barked, letting go of Moons tail.

"That's it," Moon barked at last." You turned down my offer. Now I will take the Valley by force!"

Moon raced into Flame and River but vanished. They looked around but could not see her. Then Moon reappeared behind Flame and scratched her back. Flame fell to the ground and her glowing orange fur turned dull.

"Flame!" River whimpered. She raced to Flame's side, but it was too late. She vanished into orange shards. The only thing left of her was an orange ember with a fire print on it. "You'll pay for that, you traitor!" River howled angerly.

She plunged into Moon, throwing her in the snow. Moon got back up and kicked River of the edge of the mountain. "River!" Sun cried. But a glowing light flew to the sky. It was River, she was not defeated yet.

Moon rolled her eyes. She had forgotten the powers of River's waters. River sprinted into Moon and tried to leap on her back, but Moon dug her claws into River's stomach. She landed on her back and heaved as she saw the gash in her stomach where there was no blue fur. She too disappeared into blue shards.

"No," Sun whispered, lowering her head against the cold stone. The only thing left of her was a blue ember with a water drop print on it. "You

monster. Betraying the balance, murdering your own

kin."

"I'll be happy to have no kin of mine," Moon

laughed, raising her left paw to finish her off. "Just

give up already! Your all alone, with no one left to

save you."

"I'm not losing to the enemy," Sun growled.

She grabbed the orange and blue shards and tossed

them into the air. They both showed a beaming light

that blasted Moon in the stomach, sending her across

the night sky like a shooting star. "And you will never

be welcomed here again."

Chapter 1: The Cliffs

The cave was warm and bright. Soothing sounds warmed the heart of the sleeping wolf in the center. *Follow the path that leads toward the stars.* The wolf twitched at the soft voice.

"Rain, wake up!"

"Huh?" Rain rasped. A light gray she-wolf with brown flecks of fur loomed over her.

"Bear wants us on a hunting patrol immediately," her friend informed. Rain followed the light gray she-wolf out of the den that led to the hollow cave in the mountain, seeing other wolves coming out of the tunnels made her feel more comfortable. As she and her friend raced out of the hollow, she could not stop thinking about the mysterious prophecy she heard last night. *Follow the path of stars.* What path was she supposed to follow? And how?

"About time," a wolf murmured. Rain looked at the brownish-gray wolf, a displeasing look in his brown eyes. "Thank you for fetching her, Maple." Maple stiffed proudly at her praise.

"You two will hunt along the Oasis border. You can take two more wolves with you. We can never have too much food," Bear ordered. Both Maple and Rain nodded to the wolf and bounded off to the far side of the cave where 3 wolves sat. One was gray with black fading paws and blue eyes. The other was bright white with light blue eyes. The third was the same as the first but smaller.

"Storm, Glacier, we need you on a hunting patrol," Rain informed. Both Storm and Glacier stood up from their spots but stopped when they heard the beg of the younger wolf.

15

"Can I come too?" the small wolf asked. "I promise I'll catch a lot of prey!" The young wolf leaped onto a nearby leaf and picked it up proudly, thinking it was actual prey. Storm rolled his eyes in annoyance.

"Oh, be quiet Lake. If you came with us, you would be trampled on by caribou," Storm laughed. He nudged his brother playfully in the shoulder. The patrol left Lake sitting in the cave as he pouted.

At the Oasis Border, Storm, Maple, Rain, and Glacier hunted through the small cluster of trees along the rock wall that bordered the Cliffs with the other packs. Glacier crouched down behind a squirrel. Its ears flickered in realization. Before in could escaped, Glacier grabbed its tail and sunk her claw into its hind leg.

"Thank you for your sacrifice," she prayed silently.

"Do you always pray on food like this? It's dead, it's delicious," Storm teased, with a marmot in his jaws. But Glacier just rolled her eyes, picking up the squirrel and trotting toward Rain with her head held high. She was standing over a robin.

Rain felt like something was wrong. "Has anyone seen Maple?" she asked calmly, picking up the robin. Both Glacier and Storm looked at each other and shook their heads. Suddenly, Rain noticed a mist rolling into the cluster of trees.

"Where is all this fog coming from?" Glacier asked in annoyance. As soon as she spoke, trees started to shake and leaves fell, and they heard a distant panting. They all spun around and saw Maple running towards them.

"Run!" Maple howled. Soon, they realized it was not fog rolling in, it was water!

Chapter 2: The Flood

"Good morning, Bear."

Bear squeezed through the tiny crack that led to the small den. He had finished giving the patrols that morning. "Good morning, Sky," he barked, kicking around the dust and ruble. Bear stared at the beautiful light gray she-wolf, her sky-blue eyes shining joyfully.

"Your sister was acting strange when I sent her on patrol this-" Bear was cut short when Sky looked down. Water swish beneath her paws. She turned around quickly. "A flood!" Bear gasped. Sky stared into the cave. It looked like a wave of water had already flushed into the camp, destroying bramble thickets and filling dens. Wolves were panicking, not knowing what to do.

"Quick, get everyone to the mountains before anyone gets hurt," Sky ordered. Bear nodded and raced into the water that crashed against the rocks.

"Feather? Feather?" cried a grey she-wolf. She circled in the rising water. "Have you seen Feather? I lost him when the water flushed into camp," The she-wolf had a worried look in her amber eyes.

"We'll find him, Dawn. For now, we need to get everyone to the mountains," Bear responded firmly, pointing his nose towards a tunnel just above a small overhang in the cave. Still unconvinced, Dawn followed the other wolves to the mountains.

"Sister!" Sky turned around and saw Rain pushing through the water. She could see the exhaustion in her blue eyes.

"Where are the others?" Sky demanded.

"There still at the Oasis border, but there safe," Rain explained. Sky nodded and sent her to scout the clearing before going with the other wolves. Both

Bear and Rain leaped back into the water, disappearing into the mist.

"Help!" Sky spotted a grey wolf pup, struggling in the water. It was Dawn's son, Feather. She did not realize how quickly the water was rising.

"I'm coming, Feather!" Sky howled, swimming towards the struggling wolf pup. She climbed up the steep wall and reached out to grab onto Feather. She got him by the scruff and pulled him. "Hang on, Feather?"

Bear swam up beside her and reported, "Everyone is safe except for the patrol." Sky nodded and followed him through the tunnel. She dropped Feather at his mother's paws as he curled up in a ball and tried to sleep.

"Thank you, Alpha," Dawn barked gratefully. "I don't know what we'd do without you." She bowed her head in respect towards Sky before picking up her damp, tired son and backing into the crowd of wolves

Sky bounded up a tree stump and called the cliff wolves with a mighty howl. "Wolves of the cliffs," she began. "I'm afraid that we cannot travel back to camp until most of the water is gone." Sounds of agreement and sorrow came from the cliffs wolves as Bear came up to the stump to stand by Sky.

"Sky is right. The water is too high to swim in and the pups might drown if we go back," he added firmly. Even more sounds of agreement came from the cliff wolves. It seemed like all of them agreed. Sky waited for the noise to die down before continuing to speak.

"Rain, you will take a wolf with you to the Oasis border where the afternoon hunt patrol was last seen to look for them," she barked. "For now, we shall build camp here." Rain stepped up and padded towards a dark grey wolf while the rest of the pack

started making spaces to rest.

Sky stayed where she was as Bear rounded up

the four pups and lead them to where the gammas

were sitting. She looked to the magenta sky and

barked silently, "Oh White Comet, how do I help my

pack now?"

Chapter 3: Betrayal

"Maple? Glacier? Storm?" Rain howled. Her voice echoed in the distant hills. The water had died down at the border area. She had led Owl, a gray wolf with white flecks of fur around his face and brown eyes to where her friends were last seen.

"There scent leads to this log," Rain barked, sniffing the broken log that laid on the ground. Suddenly, they heard a howl coming from the outside of the small forest. "That must be them!" Owl followed Rain out of the forest and spotted the three wolves sitting in shade of a single spruce tree.

"Come on, if we hurry, we'll be home before sunset," Owl barked joyfully. Maple bounded towards him and nosed his cheek. "Good to see you too." Glacier came up to Rain, Storm limping behind her.

"What happened?" Rain asked worryingly. Storm limped up beside Glacier looking embarrassed. Glacier nosed his ear and smiled.

"A wave of water flushed into the forest and pushed him up against a tree and he hurt his paw," Glacier explained. No wonder why he was embarrassed. He was one of the strongest wolves in the pack. "Let's go home and get him checked out."

"Yah. Plus, I want to get back home!"

"Long ago, there were four comets," Sky began as two pups trembled eagerly in front of her. It had been three days since the flood and Sky was telling a story to the young pups. "One was the comet of fire. The second was the comet of water. The third was the comet of light, and the last was the comet of shadows."

The two energetic wolf pups wagged their tails and stomped their paws in excitement. *They must have nothing to do since everyone else is busy hunting and building sleeping areas.* Rain thought, walking past her sister.

"One of the comets wanted control over all three packs thinking it could be the elite Alpha, and so-" Sky was cut off by one of the wolf pups.

"What did it do? What did it do?" the pup asked abruptly. The other wolf pup nodded his head in agreement, eager to hear the end of the story.

"Calm down and I'll tell you," she growled softly. "The shadow comet ended up destroying two of her sisters, but the light comet was too strong. It blasted the shadow comet int to the sky and was never welcomed again."

"Now only two comets roam the night skies. You see them every Starlight when the air changes," Rain concluded, sitting next to her sister. Sky smiled at Rain as the wolf pups sat in awe.

"Want to go eat?" Sky asked pointing her nose towards a rock wall. "The last patrol brought back plenty of food." Rain nodded in approval and followed Sky towards the wall. Sky paused when she spotted Maple sitting under the shade of a spruce tree next too Owl, her mate, and Owl's mother. "Maple would you like to join us for a meal?"

"Absolutely!" Maple exclaimed. She followed Rain and Sky to the wall where prey hung, but suddenly, Rain heard the strange voice and saw nothing but darkness. *Follow the path towards stars.*

"Rain, are you well?" She opened her eyes and saw Sky leaning under her shoulder. "You blacked out for a second."

"I'm...I'm fine just tired from the night patrol," she lied, stumbling to her paws. Maple shot her a look, knowing that she was lying, but said nothing.

She and Maple stared at the temporary prey wall that curved giving shelter to the dead animals that hung from it. At the base of the wall one by one, wolves stuck their paws in a pile of sticking sap and dabbing them on the prey they caught and sticking them to the wall.

Bear sat on one side of the wall and bowed his head respectively to each wolf that passed by. As he spotted the three, he dragged down a large, brown caribou from the wall and took it over to Sky. "This looks delicious!" Maple exclaimed. She lowered her head to take a bite but was knocked in the shoulder by

Rain, reminding her the tradition of when eating with an alpha not to eat until the alpha speaks.

Sky chuckled and barked, "It's all right, Maple. You may begin." Maple licked her lips and took a bite out of the caribou. Rain did the same, feeling sweet relief wash over her. She had not eaten anything since that morning before the patrol. "But now, I must tell you the real reason why we called you here."

Both Rain and Maple looked up from their meals in curiosity. *This cannot be good*, Rain thought worryingly. Maple shifted uneasily. "The dawn patrol came back telling us where the flood water came from," Bear began, his paws shifted. Rain gave Maple

a worried glanced. "The flood was caused by the

Oasis pack."

Chapter 4: Suspicions

"It can't be," Rain whimpered.

"All we know is that Oak Alpha has a lot of explaining to do," Sky growled silently. She bared her teeth at the thought of the Oasis pack attacking her pack for no reason.

Maple took another bite out of the caribou, forcing herself to swallow. "This must be a mistake. Oak Alpha and Frost would never betray they're own daughter," Rain shouted in protest. Sky bounded over to Maple and sat next to her. She licked her ear in comfort.

Maple's head hung low. Nobody knew what she was thinking, as she got up, still staring at the ground. "I can't believe it," she barked hesitantly. Then her eyes turned from confusion to anger. "I won't believe it!" She ran off into the flooded hills, her grey fur glittering in the sunlight. Rain stood up to go after her, but Sky stepped in front of her.

"Let her go," Sky ordered calmly. Rain sat back down, her ears close to her head. Sky stared off into the flooded terrain, not knowing what to do next. "She has a lot on her mind."

"She hasn't spoken to me since yesterday."

"Hopefully, the meeting with the Alpha's will give us an explanation," Sky barked to her sister. Owl, Maple, and Bear followed them through the flooded forest. Soon she spotted an island in the center of the forest. Beyond the island, some of the tree leaves faded into white. On the other, the forest faded into rocky hills and waterfalls.

In sight, another group of wolves being led by a huge gray and brown wolf and a white wolf that looked like Maple. "I see that Oak Alpha has arrived," Bear murmured to his Alpha. He bared his teeth in fury. "He better has an explanation for the flood, or else someone is goanna lose their pelt."

Sky claimed up the slab where the grey wolf was sitting. Underneath the slab, the light grey she-wolf walked up to Maple who was talking to Owl. Maple bared her teeth at the she-wolf. *Frost must be heart broken,* Sky thought. In the corner of her eye, she could see a silver wolf climbing up the slab. He nodded to Sky and Sky turned to nod to the grey wolf, and he also nodded.

Sky let out a commanding howl, signaling to the wolves below to be silent. "The sun has risen above the mountains and the Sunrise meeting between the three packs has begun," she barked loudly, her voice firm. She glanced around and caught Bear's eye. He nodded to her, encouraging her to tell the truth about the flood. "I will start with the main problem in the cliffs. A flood has flowed through our territory, but you, Oak Alpha, should already know this."

Oak's ears twitched in confusion. "The flood water came from a hole in the rock wall between the cliffs and the Oasis packs. Some of your wolves came over to our territory and moved one of the rocks, releasing the water, flooding the cliffs, and forcing us to leave our home," Sky explained more calmly.

All the wolves looked to the speechless Alpha; the Cliff wolves glared at him. He stared down at them in anger but rested his shoulders when he saw Maple's desperate stare. "My wolves would never start war without good reason," he sighed. He looked suspiciously at two Oasis wolves. They both chuckled silently.

Suddenly, anger rose from the crowd of wolves. Sounds of threat and insult filed the air. "Wait!" Every pair of eyes turned to the short, but muscular white she-wolf. "The Sunrise meeting is supposed to be peaceful. This must not end in bloodshed!"

"My beta is right. Sky, I promise I will discuss this matter with my wolves after the meeting," Oak barked to the Alpha, but Sky just nodded, still unconvinced.

"Maybe they're trying to drive us out so they can gain our territory." Bear made his way over to

Frost. Other wolves nodded in agreement. His nose

was in the she-wolf's face. Frost stumbled to her

paws.

"We would never!" she shouted in protest. Sky

bared her teeth at her beta, warning him not to start a

fight yet. Bear backed down, a suspicious look in his

eyes. All the wolves became calmer again while

Silver Alpha, the Alpha of the White Forest, told of

his pack, but the Cliff wolves were still feeling

uneasy, and Sky could tell that the flood mystery was

not a solved just yet.

Sky climbed the slope towards their temporary camp, passing her old home. She stared inside the massive cave and noticed half of the water was gone. *There is hope,* she thought joyfully.

"How come they didn't tell the truth?" Owl barked to Maple from behind. Maple did not respond. He rubbed his nose against her cheek. "We're not going to quit until we get answers, you know that." Maple smiled but stayed silent.

Sky curled up next to her sister who was talking to Glacier. Her warm soft fur made her want to sleep all her problems away. *I will need to talk to*

43

Bear tomorrow, Sky thought, drifting off into her needed rest.

Chapter 5: Uneasy Answers

"It was like he knew who started the flood but wasn't telling us." Glacier tilted her head in confusion as she listened to Rain's story. "Now, Maple feels even worse because her own parents lied to her."

"I don't blame her. If I were in her paws, I would feel betrayed too," Glacier barked, scratching behind her ear. Rain shivered at the cold breeze. *White-blossom is coming,* she thought worryingly.

She curled her tail around her sister and smiled warmly. It was just like when they were little, when they both had no care in the world. "I can tell you and Alpha need some sleep. Good rest to you and your sister." Glacier stood up and rested her chin on Rain's head. Rain nodded in appreciation, lowering her head to the cold grass, drifting off into her dreams.

"Rain?" Rain woke to find herself laying in the in the clouds. "Rain?" The voice repeated louder. His voice like thunder.

"Who goes there? Show yourself!" Rain demanded, a trickle of fear in her voice. She spun around and saw a glittering light grey wolf. His indigo eyes glowed as he stepped forward. Rain backed away cautiously, knowing who he was.

"I am Aster, former leader of-" Aster stared, his voice calmer now.

"The cliffs," Rain barked abruptly, bowing her head in respect. She had heard of the wise, but disrespected Alpha from gammas. The stars twinkled brighter then when she had woken. Possibly because of the presence of a dead wolf.

"Listen to me, following the path of stars is the only way to defeat the Shadow Spirit," he advised.

Rain opened her mouth to speak but the Alpha shook

his head.

"Don't go!" She called to the Alpha, but he was

already gone. And she was alone in the night, once

again.

At dawn the next morning, once again, the

wolves of the cliffs gathered beneath the tree stump

where Sky and Bear stood. "Wolves of the Cliffs,"

Sky began like usual. "the water is now low enough

for us to walk and we may return home." A bolt of joy

ran through Rain. She had never been happier, and

she could tell the other wolves felt the same. Behind

her, wolves howled, gammas cheered, and pups jumped with joy.

Bear waited for the noise to die down before stepping forward. "Once we return at noon, we must do everything we can to restore camp," he informed sternly. Bear had always been more serious about protecting his pack. Sky shoved him playfully, telling him to relax. But he stiffened his shoulders even more.

Rain and Sky led the Cliff wolves through the tunnel that led towards the old camp. Instead of returning to warm dens, they returned to scattered leaves and soggy prey that laid in the water. "Get to work everyone," sky ordered. Every wolf behind her began cleaning up and Glacier disappeared into a hole next to where the gamma's stayed, obviously going to check on her herbs and liquids. Rain noticed her sister was gone and decided to talk to Maple.

"Good to be home?" Rain asked Maple, who was putting a bramble thicket back together. She nodded silently, not meeting Rain's gaze. Rain's ears flattened against her head. Was Maple not going to talk to anyone? Would she become an omega just like she was in the Oasis when she was younger?

"Rain?" Rain spun around to see Bear holding damp prey in his jaws. "I need you to take these to the White Forest border and bury them deep underground so no wolf will find them. I suggest covering them in wet moss so that no one will smell them and attempt to eat them."

Rain took the prey from him and scurried of towards the healing hole where Glacier was. *I can talk to her about my dream from last night,* she thought, but she was interrupted by a challenging howl.

"I am her father!" Oak Alpha, Frost, and a group of Oasis wolves were at the entrance facing

Sky, Bear, and a dark gray senior wolf. "I demand to speak to her." Seeing Frost baring her teeth at her sister made Rain go mad. She sped to Sky's side to defend her.

"Maple will speak when she wants to," Rain stuck her nose in Frost's face just like Bear did at the meeting, but this time, Frost didn't flinch at all. She kept staring at Rain with eyes of fire. Rain looked to Sky, waiting for an order on what to do next.

"Go get Maple, me, Bear, and Foot will keep them distracted," Sky whispered. Rain nodded, leaving her sister with the intruders. She bounded over to the tunnel where Maple was carrying soggy moss.

"Maple, your parents are ambushing us, they want to see you," Rain panted. For a moment, Maple stayed silence for moment. She whispered something under her breath. Rain could not make out what she was saying, but she could tell it was not good.

"Let's go," she barked finally, brushing past Rain towards the entrance of the cave. Rain followed without saying a word. Would Oak give them an explanation? Would it fix their relationship? Rain pushed the thought away. Right now, the main problem is getting the Oasis wolves out of their territory. And what was going on inside of Maple's head. She paused when she came face to face with Oak and Frost.

"Maple, I-" Frost began.

"You have no right to be here," Maple barked abruptly, her eyes cold and her voice harsh, showing no mercy. "I know what you two are planning."

Oak moved aside to reveal three wolves. Rain recognized two of them from the meeting and she could tell Sky new them two. All three of the wolves were grey with bright amber except for the one she did not recognize who had green eyes.

"It's not what you think," Oak began. "These three moved the rocks while they were *supposed* to be on patrol, but they moved the rocks instead, releasing the water." Both Sky and Bear looked at the three wolves in shock. "What should we do with them?"

Sky waited for Maple to answer Oak's question. When Maple noticed her, she stepped forward and barked, "Leave." The three wolves looked at each other, unsure of what she meant. "Leave and never return." The Oasis wolves escorted them away. Maple turned away before anyone else could happen.

As the Oasis wolves left the cave, cliff wolves shouted words of threat and insult. "Get back to work," Sky howled. "We have a lot to do before tomorrow night." She did not need to address them, for they already knew what the cause of the flood was.

Rain padded after Maple with the damp prey, hoping she would still talk to her. "Want to help me get rid of these?" She asked. Maple smiled warmly, a real smile this time, the one that Rain missed ever so much.

"I'd love to, and I'm sorry I blocked you out for the past few days. I just felt like you would leave me because of where I came from," Maple admitted. Rain remembered how Maple had joined the Cliffs because she was not a great swimmer and terrible at fishing. The wolves of the Oasis hated her and forced her out. When her father became Alpha, he invited her back to the Oasis, but Maple had already found her place in the Cliffs with Owl.

"I would never leave you, you're my best

friend," Rain laughed, nudging Maple's shoulder.

Rain had gained her friend once again.

Chapter 6: The Fall of the Light

"Make sure no one drinks the water on the

ground, Sorrel. If they get thirsty, they can head to the

mountain where the flood did not reach," Sky

instructed. Sorrel nodded to the alpha and bounded off

to where the gammas were resting. *Today has been*

exhausting, Sky thought. She and the pack had been

working hard all day to rebuild camp before that

night. She slumped into her old den and saw nothing

but wet brambles and scattered leaves. She lowered her head towards the stone, too tired to clean up. She felt Bear's fur brush against her as he began to fall asleep next to her.

Sky stood at the entrance to her den underneath the ledge when she noticed Rain shoving Feather through the entrance to the cave. Dawn pushed her way through the healing hole towards Rain in anger. "What's the matter?" Sky demanded. She stared intensely at Feather, already knowing he did something wrong.

"This wolf pup was running through the cliffs without an escort," Rain informed firmly.

Sky looked to her sister and back at the wolf pup. "Don't you know how dangerous it is to be adventuring in The Valley?" The wolf pup shifted his paws, ready to receive a punishment.

"No, he doesn't," Dawn growled. She pushed Feather behind her with her paw, protecting her son. "He's not even 2 lunars old yet!"

"He will be tonight, so he must assist Glacier with herbs and liquids. He won't become the lota though," Sky barked, pointing her nose to where

Dawn just came from. "Even though the gammas are supposed to be watching him, he did sneak off, and he is old enough to take responsibility." Dawn opened her mouth to protest but Rain gave her a look telling her to obey, taking her sister's side.

Dawn turned away, furious with Sky's decisions. She had never been so hostile towards Sky before. She had always been loyal to the Cliffs Alpha. "Go on now, you got work to do," Rain ordered, nudging Feather towards the healing hole where white, glittering ferns grew. The pup scampered off without a word. "Those ferns are a sign of Red-

Blossom ending." She looked at the frost ferns, worry in her eyes.

"We still have time," Sky barked, trying to calm down her sister. Red-Blossom had always been sacred to the wolves of The Valley because it gave them a chance to prepare for the coldest, and most unforgiving season of all: White-Blossom.

Later that evening, the wolves of the Cliffs sat in a circle around Sky and Glacier. Bear and Rain stood at the head of the crowd. "Tonight, the winds change, and the birds fly south as we welcome White-Blossom," Sky howled to the wolves.

61

Glacier was silent for a moment. Her ear twitched because of the jay feathers behind it that she wore on special occasions. Then, she let out a howl to summon her pack. The wolves joined her as two comets appeared in the night sky. A white one and a violet one. At first, they circled but then, they bounced off each other.

"They're fighting each other!" A pup whimpered; her ears flat against her head and her tail covering her shaking paws. Sky had forgotten that this some of the pups first Starcross

"That's what they do," Sky insisted. The two comets continued to bounce of each other until the white comet disappeared. All the gammas gasped, and a wolf covered Lake's eyes with her tail.

"The shadow has won!" wolf cried.

"How could this happen?"

"This is no good!"

"Why has the light surrender?" Glacier asked in worry. Sky didn't answer. She stood staring at the sky, so many things going on in her head. If the light has been defeated and The Valley was in the paws of the shadow spirit now, they were domed.

Finally, Sky looked upon her wolves, fear and confusion in their faces. "I'd like to speak with my advisors please. Gravel, lead everyone back to the cave." Gravel nodded and took the wolves through the tunnel.

Rain paced back and forth in the Alpha den and Glacier stomped her paw on the ground, trying to think of what to do. Sky looked to her sister and asked, "Rain, what is wrong?"

She nudged Rain's shoulder worryingly. "I had a dream a few nights ago," she barked forcingly. All the others stared at her. Sky new that few wolves had special dreams like thetas do. "and it was a prophecy from Aster Alpha."

"That tree-minded squirrel?" Bear bared his teeth in disgust.

"I forgave him, and I know you will to," Sky barked calmly. She gave him a look to keep quiet so that Rain could continue.

"He said that someone had to defeat the wrath of shadows, and if he came to *me,* I thought that I was the wolf in the prophecy," Rain explained, shifting her paws uneasily. *How does a wolf defeat an invincible spirit?* Sky thought. She had forgotten that prophecies did not always make sense.

"Then you must defeat it," Glacier stood up with serious look on her face. All of them looked at her, puzzled and confused. "If it's the only way to save our pack, then do it."

Chapter 7: Moon

That night, Rain thought about what Glacier said. How would she, and ordinary wolf, defeat an invincible spirit. The light spirit would be able to, but it has mercy on the shadow spirit. She rolled around in her sleep, trying to push the thought away as she dozed off.

"Hello, Rain." Rain looked up from her paws. She felt cold stone under her pads as she realized she was no longer in the wolf den, but at Sunisles.

"Is that you Aster?" She rasped. But instead of seeing the wise former alpha, she saw a she-wolf with fur as black as night. She stepped forward her eye were deep violet.

"Before you ask, I am Moon," the wolf barked. Rain stood up in curiosity. She had never heard of Moon before, and the gammas always told of the wolves before them. The names had been passed down for generations. Moon was an odd name to have.

Before Rain could ask any questions, Moon stepped forward and an image appeared on the ground. It was an image of Bear being announced as beta. "Do you ever feel like you should have been chosen as beta?" Moon asked Rain.

"A little. Bear will do anything to please and protect the pack, but he is loyal and brave," Rain barked. She was thankful to be helping her sister with important decisions.

"That is all I need to know," Moon barked as the image vanished. She padded away into the Ancestor Stream that ran around Sunisles.

"But why? Who even are you?"

"Just know that I am going to change your life, forever," Moon laughed. Rain felt a paw on her shoulder jolt her awake. It was Glacier waking her up

"Sky wants us to go to Sunisles for a meeting with the Alphas," Glacier informed. Rain nodded; she did not say a word about her dream.

The patrol trotted silently through the forest. Instead of seeing the caring sister she always knew, she saw a stern, fierce Alpha, fighting for her pack. Rain could tell she was serious about this meeting.

"Are you sure Bear will be okay looking after camp?" Rain asked in worry.

"Don't be ridiculous! If the pack can survive without both of us, they can survive without one of us," Sky insisted. Sky had a point about the wolves being fine, but Rain was really worried about Bear. What Moon said last night made her feel uneasy about leaving Bear alone.

"Welcome Silver Alpha, Sky Alpha." Oak looked calmer than the last time they saw him. The alphas sat in a circle instead of on the slab since they were not addressing anyone. The betas and thetas gossiped about the trouble going on in their territories until the alphas were ready.

"The defeat of the Light Spirit means a dark future for The Valley," Silver began. His fur was light grey, like his name, and he had unusual eyes. One was amber yellow, and one was blue. "That's why if anyone has *any* dreams from the ancestors, tell your alphas immediately."

Guilt washed over Rain as she heard "any." Neither Rain nor Sky would lie to each other. But she still had so many questions about her dream. Rain looked to the left of Silver. There sat a white she-wolf with green eyes and tan flecks of fur around her face. She looked nervous. Rain had never seen her before either. The she-wolf had a blue feather behind her ear, so she was a theta.

"Are you listening?" Frost shouldered Rain. Rain bared her teeth in response and continued to listen to the alphas. Rain had always been despised by Frost, but she did not know why.

After the meeting, Rain padded over to Glacier. "Who is the she-wolf standing next to Silver? I've never seen her before."

"Oh, that's Cloud. She is shy and does not really talk to anyone since the theta who trained her died of old age. She was always with Marsh, so she only trust is Ash, the White Forest beta," Glacier answered. Rain remembered the wise theta that was an ally of Sky.

"You should meet her," Sky barked from behind. She sat proudly next to Glacier. She was obviously in a better mood then the journey here.

Rain made her way over to the white she-wolf, who was sitting behind Siver when he was talking to Frost. "You must be Cloud," she smiled warmly. She stumbled to her paws.

"How did you know?" Cloud flinched. She became more scared. *Strange,* Rain thought.

On the way back, grey clouds covered the sky and rain poured over them. The patrol traveled through the frosted evergreen when a gray wolf came running towards Sky.

"Sky! Sky!" The wolf hollered. It was Storm! But what was he doing all the way out here?

"Storm, what are you doing here?" Sky demanded, knowing it was not good news.

Storm's eyes filled with terror as he blurted out, "Bear is dead!"

Chapter 8: Revenge

Every inch of pride in Sky was gone now.

"How?" Rain demanded. Sky felt like her heart was torn into two. Bear was not just a beta, but she loved him.

"The three wolves front the Oasis attacked him. We were patrolling the mountains near the White Forest border when they ambushed us. They clearly had gotten stronger since they were banished, too,"

Storm explained. Rain followed him into their territory, but Sky was lost in thought.

"Come on, Sky!" Glacier pushed Sky in the direction where Rain and Storm were going. Sky ran through the forest; she ran like she was leading her pack into battle. She ran so fast that the whole Forest was a green blur. She didn't even care for the pouring rain that ran down her side and dripped on to the grass.

"We have them pinned," Storm informed. Sky nodded and padded to where Owl was pining a wolf to the ground. A scratch was on his hind leg.

"Why?" Sky asked the grey wolf. He silently glared at the alpha. Sky rose with anger. She slashed her paw across his face. "Why have you done this to our pack?" She spoke more aggressive this time.

"Your pack is pathetic! The wolves of The Valley are pathetic," he responded forcefully. "All you care about is peace and loyalty. But one day, everything will change, and The Valley will be destroyed." He scrunched his nose in pain from the scratch.

"It's more then you'll ever be," Rain growled. "Storm, Owl, and I will escort them away to the

Beyonds." The wolves stared in horror. They thought they would get a little of their mercy.

Sky let the wolf go with the others and barked, "If you are found in our territory again, you will be caught and killed." She saw the three wolves shiver in fear when they heard her.

Sky made her way to the Ancestor Stream that ran around Sunisles, were dying wolves laid on their journey to the stars. Bear floated in the water, his mouth slightly opened and breathless. "You were the most brave and loyal beta I could have," she whispered, pressing her chin on his head.

She pushed him down the stream that led to a frozen river leading to the Beyonds. It was time for her to choose a new beta.

That night, Sky stood at the edge of the overhang in the cave. The water was gone at last and the wolves of the Cliffs gathered beneath her. Glacier stood underneath the overhang waiting for everyone to be silent.

"Bear was a noble beta and would have made a great Alpha for the Cliffs. Now it is time to choose a new beta," Sky was quiet for a moment before continuing. Then she looked down at her sister and stared into her indigo eyes. "Rain, you have proven yourself as a leader." Rain climbed to the ledge proudly as wolves congratulated her.

"Thank you, sister," Rain barked, pressing her nose against Sky ear. She turned towards the wolves. "I promise to serve you all as beta till the day of my death." Finally, she howled to the Cliffs wolves. The wolves joined her as they remembered the spirit of Bear.

Sky slumped into her den, tired and lonely. She felt a wolf lay next to her. At first, she thought it was Bear. Then she scented Rain. "Goodnight sister," Rain whispered. Sky responded with a low moan, falling asleep with her sister by her side.

The next morning, Sky woke to see light coming from the opening of the den. The sharp edges in the cave casted shadow as she got up.

"Your finally awake." Glacier was sitting in the corner of the den smiling. "I almost thought you were in a coma."

"What time is it," Sky asked, blinking rapidly.

"It's nearly noon."

Chapter 9: The Trail

A blood curdling howl came from the Alpha
den. "How could I have slept in for half of the day!"
Sky bolted out of her den frantically, her fur was
messy, and she had been miserable all night. *I knew I
should not had let her sleep in,* Rain thought.

"I never oversleep!" Sky barked, sticking her nose in Glacier's face. Rain padded up to her sister. The first day of being beta and she had already done something wrong!

"It was my fault. I ordered everyone to let you sleep in after what happened last night," Rain barked, looking down at her paws.

"Thank you, sister, but I must care for my pack before you care for me," Sky sighed. "Did you send out the-"

"Dawn patrol? Yes, I joined it myself. We had time for hunting too," Rain barked proudly, pointing her nose to the prey wall. She was right, the prey wall was filled, and all the wolves were feasting.

Sky nosed Rain's ear respectfully. "I knew you were the right wolf for the job," she whispered. She padded towards the prey wall to speak with the phis, and Rain knew why.

That afternoon, Rain's job was to assess the two psi to make sure they were good hunters and ready to finish training. "I want both of you to go on solo hunting missions," Rain began. "Thorn, you will hunt along the forever freeze. The prey in the White Forest will already want to come here where its warmer." The young grey wolf nodded and went off towards the White Forest alone.

"Can I take the cougar route?" The white wolf pup asked. She had flecks of brown on her face and her blue eyes were bulging out of her head.

Rain couldn't resist. "All right. You can take the Cougar Route, Floral," Rain sighed. Floral perked up and skipped away towards the sandy trail. "Don't make me regret it!" Floral didn't look back. She kept skipping without a care in the world.

"Rain! Rain!" Thorn raced towards the beta, grass clinging to his fur. "I found something you need to see."

Rain followed Thorn by a river called the Forever Freeze. It never thawed even in the hottest Warm-Blossom. The territory on the other side of the river was White Forest, which was mysteriously always white as snow.

"Look," Thorn pointed is paws to a trail of paw prints. But they glowed black and violet in the mud. Rain recognized those colors. The colors of the shadow spirit.

87

Chapter 10: The Loner

"So, you're saying the Shadow Spirit has already come?" Glacier's light blue eyes filled with fear. Every wolf in the Valley coward at the mention of the name. The Shadow Spirit was evil and longed for power.

"But looked at all the prey I caught!" Thorn held up the heavy pheasant and two hares laid at his paws. Rain smiled proudly. For a little bit, she had been Thorn's sigma and trained him when he was just starting out. She could tell she trained Thorn well.

"Hmp," Floral stumped her paw on the ground. "I could've gotten more then you if you hadn't dragged me away." She held a plump, but small marmot.

"You will have time to do your assessment later," Glacier barked calmly, pressing her nose behind Floral's ear.

Night came and the stars were dim. Sky creped out of the cave and into the hills. She told Thorn, Floral, Glacier, and Rain to keep the Shadow Spirits

89

arrival a secret. The night area was still damp from rain and un-promised snow. Then she saw them, glowing black paw prints, exactly how Thorn described them. She followed them along the Forever Freeze and into the White Forest. Feeling uneasy exploring different territory, she kept going.

Sky followed the paw prints for a while before they lead to a stop, she did not notice the sun was beginning to rise. "I should head back now," she sighed. Disappointed and tired. She turned around, not realizing she was on a ledge.

Suddenly, when she turned around, a large, black wolf jumped out of the rising sun. Sky stumbled back and fell to the ground at the bottom of the cliff.

Sky tried to pull herself up, but she was too weak and hungry. She closed her eyes as she felt teeth grip her scruff. Was it the black wolf? Was it a White Forest wolf? Or worse, a cougar or bear? She tried not to think about it, letting the mysterious creature drag her across the White Forest, and all at once, snow began to fall.

"No, she is still breathing." Sky opened her eyes. She was lying in the healing hole on a slab in

91

the center of the burrow. A grey jay was laid next to her. Glacier was talking to an unfamiliar wolf. He was a large, dark grey wolf with amber eyes.

"Look who finally woke up," the wolf chuckled. His yellow eyes burned into Sky's as she clenched her cheeks in embarrassment.

"Leave her alone! She took a hard fall you know," Glacier barked defensively. Glacier had always been protective of Sky because of how she was teased when she grew up. "Sky, this is Sashien. He rescued you when you were in *another* pack's territory." Glacier gave her a look of disappointment, telling her they needed to talk later.

Sky pulled herself up to her paws. She was even more embarrassed to look weak in front of a loner. "Thank you, Sashien, we are in debt," she barked bowing her head.

"Please, call me Cobalt. That is what they called me at the enclosure," Sashien barked, bowing his head in return. Sky smiled slightly. She had never met a loner like him before. It was instinct to chase out a loner or even kill it because most loners were tricksters and selfish.

"Are you from the Beyonds? I have never seen you in the other packs before," Sky asked, tilting her head to one side. Sashien began to tell the wolves about how he escaped a place far away where "tallhares" kept other wolves like him in cages. Every time he said "tallhares" he squinted his eyes in disgust.

Both Sky and Glacier sat in interest. They had never heard of humans before. "What are tallhares?" Sky asked abruptly. "Are they harmful?"

"Tallhares are furless, creatures who have odd anatomy," Sashien responded. "They walk on their hind legs and their claws are very short."

Both Glacier and Sky nodded. "One thing is for sure," Glacier stood up to meet face-to-face with him. "We owe you for saving our Alpha."

"I would like to join your pack."

Chapter 11: Instinct

Rain speed out of the entrance to camp. She had gone looking for Sky in the middle of the night when she heard she went missing. One of the wolves guarding the cave entrance told her a wolf came to them with Sky passed out on his back. She ran up to the Storm, who was guarding the Healing Hole.

"Where is my sister?" She demanded. Her ears were twitching rapidly.

"She's inside, but you can't go in-" Storm started to talk but Rain wasn't having it. Before he could finish, Rain darted down the tunnel. She saw Sky talking to Glacier and a wolf she did not recognize.

"Rain, I'm glad you could make it to our little meeting," Sky barked joyfully. She was in better shape then she thought. "This is Sashien," The grey wolf padded up to Rain and bowed his head in respect. "The newest member of our pack." Sky gave her a pleading look, hoping she would aprove.

Sashien perked up. He lifted his head and smiled. "I won't let you down, Alpha."

Rain trotted back and forth in front of the Wind Ledge. She had been contemplating on wither to trust Sashien or not. He came out of nowhere and asked to join the pack without any question? He also didn't try to challenge Sky for leadership at all like most loners.

Sky was getting ready to announce Sashien's arrival to the pack on the Wind Ledge. She climbed to the top of the ledge and let out a confident howl to summon the Cliff wolves. "I, Sky Alpha, would like to be the first wolf to welcome our newest member of the pack," she began. She flicked her bushy tail, gesturing for Sashien to sit next to her. "Sashien, you will no longer hold your birth name, for you will gain the name Bolt, because of your tallhare name."

Bolt bowed his head towards the Alpha. "I pledge to protect and serve this pack till the day of my death." He let out a final howl to conclude the

meeting. The cliff wolves joined him, including Rain.
She did not trust Bolt, but it was tradition to howl
with a pack member.

While Sky watched over camp, Rain had to
teach Bolt how to hunt and fight. She led him to a
place deep in the mountains where little trees grew.

"Now," Rain began. "Show me how you hunt."
Rain pointed her nose towards a caribou. She wanted
to test him on what he knew about the wildlife in The
Valley. He had a frazzled look on his face as he
walked up to the caribou while Rain stayed behind a
bush.

Bolt walked up to the caribou without crouching or sniffing the air. *What in the name of White comet is he doing?* Rain thought. The caribou noticed Bolt and jumped up. It started kicking and crying as Bolt yowled, "Help me!"

Rain rolled her eyes and dashed to the rescue. She clawed at the caribou's thigh and bit its leg. The caribou fell to the ground, covered in scratches. "What was that?" Rain scolded. Her blue eyes like ice. She bared her teeth at him, wondering if she should hunt him instead.

"I don't know! Usually, food just lies on the ground!" He cried. Rain stepped back, forcing herself not to get too upset.

"This is going to take longer than I thought," she murmured under her breath. She sat Bolt down near a broken log. She wanted to know why he wasn't the hunter she thought he would be. He was from the Beyonds. There should be more prey there since there isn't that many wolves beyond The Valley.

"I'm a terrible hunter, aren't I?" Bolt asked. His head was hung low in shame and he flattened his ears against his head.

"Not the best. You just need more practice," Rain barked calmly. But he was right. She just did not want to admit it. Bolt smiled warmly, staring into Rain's eyes. They were kind and soft like a doe. Rain spotted a chickadee pecking at the dirt for seeds and insects. It was hungry, but her pack was hungry too. "Watch me do it."

She jumped on it before it could fly away. She wanted to teach Bolt how to hunt birds because they were the cliffs natural prey. Rain sank her teeth into the bird's white feathers and carried it over to Bolt.

"Seer? Esry!" Rain muffled with the bird in her jaws. She dropped it at his paws as Bolt stared in awe.

"That. Was. Amazing!" Bolt sniffed the chickadee quickly. "This smells much better than the hare droppings at the encloser!"

Rain blushed at the compliment. She picked up the bird and buried it in front of the log. Shaking dirt from in between her claws, she began to teach Bolt how to hunt.

By the end of the day, the two managed to catch the caribou, the chickadee, and two more birds. Rain was impressed by how fast Bolt had learned and by his fighting skills. He nearly bowled Rain over, leaving a scratch on her ankle.

"How did it go?" Sky trotted towards the pair of wolves. "By the looks of it, he is doing well." Sky sniffed the prey and raised her head proudly. Take these to the prey wall. The gammas will be pleased."

"The what?" Bolt tilted his head in confusion. Rain forgot that he was new to the ways of the pack.

"I will show him," Rain insisted. She wanted to know more about Bolt. Rain led Bolt to the prey wall. There was less prey than usual now that White-blossom was here.

"Wow," Bolt stared at the wall that made every wolf's mouth water. He licked his lips and barked, "I've never seen this much food in my life!" Rain dipped her paw in the pile of sap and dabbed in on the caribou, showing Bolt how they save prey. He did the same with the bird.

"Would you look at that," a wolf rasped, limping over to Rain and Bolt. "The newbie is fitting in just fine." The she-wolf was grey with a long scar that went down her ear and across her back.

"I'm goanna share this with the gammas." The gamma limped away with the bird in her jaws. That is what the wolves called Bolt, "the newbie." Even though Bolt did not show any emotion, Rain knew he wanted to shout in protest.

Rain shouldered Bolt playfully. "I think you're going to fit in just fine."

Chapter 12: New Arrivals

Sky rested next to Maple in the sunlight on the outside of the cave where the snow from a few nights before had melted. She kept glancing at Maple's stomach, knowing something was wrong. Sky knew it was rude, but she was too curious.

Maple caught Sky's eye and chuckled. "Oh, I guess you might as well know," she began joyfully. "I'm... I'm having Owl's pups!" A shock of delight rushed inside of Sky to know that they were expanding their pack. She rested her nose on Maple's head in respect.

"Congratulations!" Sky barked. Suddenly, a thought popped into her mind. "You know that after the next Sunrise Meeting, you will be convicted to the camp for a while. And after that, the Healing Hole."

"Don't remind me," Maple murmured, rolling her eyes. Sky knew that Maple longed to run freely through the hills without a care in the world.

Leaving Maple in the sunlight, Owl and Maple reminded Sky of her and Bear. She had never been so lonely before because he was always by her side. They grew up together. She glanced up at the magenta sky, wondering if Bear was up there. Stars were beginning to show through the clouds and the evening patrol was beginning to leave out. Rain stood at the head of the patrol talking to Thorn.

"Sister, a word," Sky asked abruptly. Rain nodded, leaving Thorn with the rest of the wolves. "Instead of leading patrol, I want you to assess Floral again. As for Thorn, his days as a psi are over."

"Of course," Rain responded. Following the order, she trotted towards a den where Floral would most likely be.

Sky led the patrol through the hills along the two borders, staying alert for any cougars or lynx. "Thorn tell me what you smell," Sky barked. Thorn sniffed the air and his nose pointed behind Sky and Ice. "Odd," he barked silently. "I scented this when-"

Suddenly, Sky heard a cracking from behind. A tree was about to fall on top of Ice! Ice turned around, her eyes wide with fear. Sky dashed towards Ice and shoved her out of the way of the tree. Dust flew everywhere, revealing Sky's tail trapped under the tree, barely missing her hind legs

Sky howled in pain. "Get Glacier!" she rasped. Thorn raced into the tree towards the cave, leaving the Alpha in pain.

"Sky!" Rain sped to her sister's side. "What happened here?" Sky opened her mouth to speak, but nothing came out. She was badly hurt. Ice bounded to her side and pressed her nose behind Sky's ear.

"It doesn't matter how it happened you buffoon!" Ice growled. "Get her some help." Glacier pushed her way through the wolves with some wet leaves in her jaws. She dropped them when she saw Sky. Half on her tail was stuck under the tree, while Ice was covered in dust and scratches.

"Ok. Foot, Ice, Rain, and I will lift the tree. When the tree is high enough, Sky will have to run away as fast as she can." Foot, Rain, and Ice followed Glacier behind the tree. Glacier stuck her nose underneath the fallen tree and pushed upward as the others did the same.

Soon, Sky felt her tail being released from the tree and darted away as fast as she could. Her tail was covered in bark and patches of fur were snagged.

"Hey! Look at this!" Foot called. Rain followed Foot to the hollow tree stump while Ice and Glacier helped Sky get up. They all looked inside and saw purple goo, seeping into the grass. It had dissolved the inside of the stump like acid.

"It's coming for us," Glacier barked hesitantly.

"*What* is coming for us?" Foot asked in worry. Sky and Rain looked at each other and knew what she meant. Glacier did not answer. She kept staring at the purple goo.

"We should head back."

Sky laid in healing hole on the slab in the center. Her tail was still flattened but most of her fur grew back after a few days. "You're lucky Alpha. One inch closer and you would never be able to walk again." Glacier was carrying cranberries in her mouth while Feather held a marmot. He laid the marmot next to Sky.

"Thank you, Feather. I think you have learned your lesson. In a couple of days, you will start your training," Sky barked calmly. Feather jumped in joy and raced up through the tunnel without saying a word.

"Here, you have not eaten anything since yesterday," Glacier insisted, pushing the marmot closer. Sky took a bite of the marmot and felt sweet relief wash over. Glacier was right. Sky had been so focused on still helping her pack, she had no intention to eat.

"Glacier?" Sky asked the Theta. She turned her head towards Sky, knowing what she was going to ask. "I... I think it's time we tell the pack about the shadow spirit."

Glacier nodded slightly. "I'll tell Rain that we'll announce it at Moonrise. That way, everyone will not be skittish all day," she responded. Trotting away, Sky knew that what she had decided would bring panic to the wolves of the cliffs, but it had to be done.

The Cliff wolves gathered around the Wind Ledge where Rain, Glacier, and Sky stood. "Wolves of the Cliffs," Sky began. "I bring grave news. As you know, the loss of Bear and the fallen tree are not accidents." The wolves glanced at each other anxiously. "The shadow spirit has arrived in the Cliffs."

Chapter 13: Deserving

Rain padded into the wolves' den after Sky's announcement. Wolves had been shaky on their way to their sleeping courters. Rain glanced around, looking for a specific wolf. She stepped among the sleeping wolves as quietly as possible when she saw two of them. It was Maple and Owl, huddled in the moonlight that showed through the entrance of the den. It was Bolt who she was looking for. But she did not see him.

"Hey, Sorrel?" Rain pawed at the brownish-grey wolf's shoulder. He jolted awake immediately.

"What? I'm trying to sleep!" Sorrel whispered angrily. He blinked sleep from his eyes. "And I'm not the only one."

"Where is Bolt?" Rain demanded silently. She bent down towards the older wolf, showing him, she would not leave without an answer.

"He left with Gravel on patrol. Now leave me be!" Sorrel turned over and began to snore again. Rain looked around but could not see Bolt or Gravel. Realizing she had nothing to do, she slumped into the Alpha's den and curled up in a cluster of leaves and began to sleep.

Rain stood up in the darkness of Sunisles. This was where she met Moon many nights ago, and she could tell someone was watching her. Rain stepped towards the rustling bush beside the slab.

"Hello, Moon," she barked. As she predicted, the black she-wolf leapt out of the bush and chuckled.

"You are quite the tracker, Rain. And you can thank me for that new position of yours," she barked, brushing past Rain. Rain soon noticed that Moon had glowing purple eyes. *It cannot be, Rain thought.*

"You!" Rain gasped. She leaped in front of Moon blocking her path. "You're the reason our home is being threatened! You're the reason my sister was injured badly!"

Moon was as small as a squirrel now. Her tail between her shaking legs, her ears against her head. Rain turned away from the black she-wolf full of fury. No longer filled with curiosity, but rage.

"Rain, wait! We can still gain power over The Valley," Moon begged. "All who have doubted us will be feared by us, feared by you."

Rain shook her head and barked back, "Being feared is not the way to gain respect. If you had not shattered the other comets, you would know that." Rain's claws dug into the grass. She did not want to be like Moon, and she would not. "I want nothing to do with you, Shadow Spirit." She bared her teeth at the black wolf angerly as she bounded away from her horrible nightmare.

Chapter 14: Remembrance

Sky sat at the top of the mountain above the camp cave, gazing upon The Valley. Snow covered the trees and birds flew above her. Prey was being hunted less and it was officially White-Blossom. Rain climbed up the stones quickly. She paused a couple of feet before reaching the top, watching the sun rise over the other side of The Valley. Sky flicked her bushy tail, gesturing for Rain to sit next to her.

"It's beautiful, isn't it," Rain barked silently, staring into the rising sun.

"Yes," Sky responded, not losing sight of the sun. "Bear would always come up here every time a wolf passed. I never understood why, but now I do."

"You miss him, don't you?" Rain tilted her head towards the fading stars.

Sky's voice was sappy. "I do. I really do," she sighed. Rain pressed her nose against Sky's shoulder in sympathy.

"I...I met the Shadow Spirit in a dream," Rain barked abruptly. Sky's ears twitched when she looked to sister. "She wanted to turn me into a tyrant."

"You're not going to follow in her paw steps, right?" Sky asked.

"Sky, you know I would never. The Shadow Spirit is history to me, as it should be," Rain chuckled, shouldering her sister's side. The sun was above the mountains now, and Sky felt the smooth stone under her pads. She realized her sister was stronger and more resilient then she thought, and more certain than ever that she was going to be a great Alpha.

Sky saw Rain perk up when another wolf bounded up the mountain. "Alpha, Beta, I brought you something." It was Bolt carrying a dove in his jaws. His dark grey fur was a speck in the bright green leaves on the frosted spruce trees. "Oh, did I interrupt something?" Bolt dropped the dove at his paws and started to back away.

"No. Never be afraid to approach me, Bolt," Sky barked calmly. Bolt nodded and climb down the mountain towards camp. Sky followed Rain's gaze towards the wolf in training. "You like him, don't you?"

"What?" Rain nearly fell over when her sister mentioned Bolt.

"Come on, little sister. I've known ever since you took him hunting that day," Sky laughed. "And I don't blame you." Sky shouldered Rain playfully.

Rain stiffened. "Sure, he's loyal, generous, charming..." Rain's voice trailed off, but she caught herself in her thoughts. "But I'm not in love with him." Sky gave her a look, knowing she was lying for the sake of her reputation. She chuckled under her breath as a swift breeze blew against her chest, ruffling up her fur.

"Rain?" Sky asked, staring into the magenta sky where the sun had been. "Promise me that you won't lead leadership go to your head?"

Rain stared at her sister in shock. *Was the question really that offensive,* Sky thought in worry. She showed no emotion when Rain sighed, "Yes."

Sky felt a soft, sweet feeling when she looked over Rain's shoulder. There sat a glittering, brownish-grey wolf and knew exactly who it was. She stared into his glowing brown eyes. Sky did not say anything, soaking in the moment as their journey of

leadership had only just begun.

Author's Note

I like to think of myself as an artist in all genres. Art, photography and music. Most importantly I love being outdoors and writing until my mind goes up in flames. If there was an Avatar the Last Airbender musical I'd totally play Katara. A lot of stuff in this story is made up but it teaches you that you make your own chooses.

"You can't make decisions based on fear and the possibility of what might happen." -Michelle Obama

Fun Fact #1: The character Foot is inspired by my grandfather and retired police officer. He's a lovable senior wolf who loves giving the pups treats and telling them stories.

Fun Fact #2: The Cliffs camp is actually an abandoned mine. That's why there are so many dens and tunnles.

Made in the USA
Monee, IL
30 July 2020